First published in Switzerland under the title *Hoppel und der Osterhase.*

No part of this publication may be reproduced in whole or in part, or stored in a
retrieval system, or transmitted in any form or by any means, electronic,
mechanical, photocopying, recording, or otherwise, without written permission
of the publisher. For information regarding permission, write to North-South
Books Inc., 1123 Broadway, Suite 800, New York, NY 10010.

ISBN 0-590-06031-7

Copyright © 1993 by Nord-Süd Verlag AG.
English translation copyright © 1993 by North-South Books Inc.
All rights reserved. Published by Scholastic Inc., 555 Broadway,
New York, NY 10012, by arrangement with North-South Books Inc.

12 11 10   1 2/0

Printed in the U.S.A.   14

First Scholastic printing, March 1997

Hopper's Easter Surprise

By Kathrin Siegenthaler and Marcus Pfister

Illustrated by Marcus Pfister

Translated by Rosemary Lanning

SCHOLASTIC INC.

New York   Toronto   London   Auckland   Sydney

Hopper was sitting in his hollow, thinking. "Will I always be an arctic hare, Mama?" he asked.

"Of course," said his mother with a smile. "You'll grow bigger and stronger, but you'll always be a hare."

"I wish I could be another animal once in a while," said Hopper, leaping nimbly over his mother's back. "I want to fly like a bird."

"That would be fun," said his mother, "but I'm afraid you can't. Just think what hares can do, though. No other animal can leap or turn somersaults as well as you."

Hopper followed his mother to the edge of the high plains and gazed down into the valley below.

"Do all hares look alike, Mama?" Hopper asked. "I hope not. I don't want to look like all the others."

"You don't look like all the others. One of your ears has a beautiful blue tip. When summer comes, your fur will turn brown, and you'll look more like the hares who live down there. The Easter bunny has brown fur too."

"The Easter bunny? Who's he?"

"The Easter bunny is someone very special. I have heard many wonderful stories about him. They say he can run faster than the wind, and when he ducks down into a hollow or hides in the undergrowth, not even the falcon with its sharp eyes can find him. That's why no one has ever seen him."

"What else do they say about him, Mama?" asked Hopper eagerly.

"He is very brave. Neither the fox nor the wolf frightens him. And every year at Easter he collects eggs from the henhouses and cleverly carries them home. Then he decorates the eggs and hides them for children to find. There, now I've told you everything I know."

"I want to be an Easter bunny!" cried Hopper, rushing away.

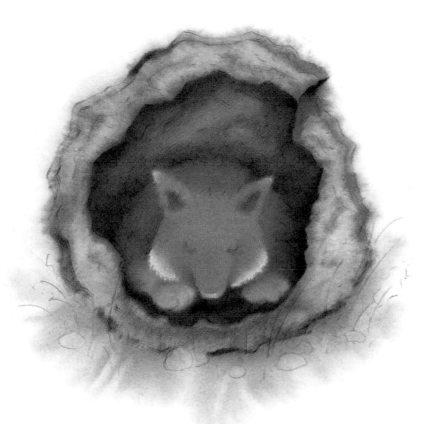

But after a few moments he stopped. "Just how do you become an Easter bunny?" he wondered. "Let me think. What did Mama say? You have to be brave, and you mustn't be afraid of the fox."

So Hopper went bounding through the forest, looking for a fox. At last he found one. The fox was sleeping in a hollow log. He had expected a fox to be more dangerous than this. Fast asleep, it looked quite harmless.

If only Mama could see how brave I'm being, thought Hopper.

Suddenly the fox leaped out and tried to
grab Hopper.

He had picked up the little hare's scent
from a long way off and was only pretending
to be asleep. Hopper just managed to jump
out of the way. He turned a quick somersault
and ran for his life.

Hopper raced into a thick clump of long grass and crouched down as low as he could. He was out of breath and his heart was pounding. He certainly couldn't run faster than the wind, like the Easter bunny.

But hiding was good enough. The fox gave up looking for him and trotted away.

"Oh dear! It's hard work being an Easter bunny," sighed Hopper.

He crept quietly out of the long grass and hopped into a meadow. Hopper couldn't believe his eyes. A brown hare was sitting right in front of him.

"Hello," said the brown hare.

"Hello," said Hopper shyly. "Are you the Easter bunny?"

"The Easter bunny? Who's he? I'm just an ordinary hare."

"That's a pity," said Hopper. Then he told the brown hare everything he knew about the Easter bunny. "I want to be an Easter bunny myself," he added.

"What a great idea," said the brown hare. "Come on, let's go over to the henhouse. It can't be that hard to carry a few eggs around."

Once inside, the two young hares explained to the hens
that they wanted to be Easter bunnies and needed some eggs.

"Of course you can have some!" cackled a kindly hen.
"Here, take these—one for you and one for you. But mind you
don't drop them."

"Don't worry. We'll be careful. And thanks a lot."

"Come on," said Hopper. "Let's take these back to my mama. She's sure to know the best way to decorate them."

They walked very carefully, but the climb up to the high plains was much harder than they had expected.

Just before they reached the top, disaster struck. Hopper took a tumble and the brown hare tripped over him. Both the eggs were smashed.

Hopper's mother tried to comfort them when they got home. "Don't be sad, children," she said. "While you were away, someone brought a present for you."

Hopper and his friend stared at the beautiful white egg tied with a red ribbon.

"Is it from the Easter bunny?" asked Hopper.

"Yes it is," said his mother. "He thought you might like to decorate it yourself. You're very tired now, but in the morning I will show you how to paint it."

Then the brown hare curled up close to Hopper and soon they were both fast asleep, dreaming of all the lovely patterns they could paint on their special Easter egg.